THIS BOOK BELONGS TO

Aleva Shah

361 00409 5

Published by Purnell Books, Paulton, Bristol,
BS18 5LQ, a member of the BPCC group of companies.
Reprinted 1983
Made and printed in Great Britain by Purnell and Sons
(Book Production) Ltd, Paulton, Bristol.

NODDY
AT THE SEASIDE

BY

Enid Blyton

CONTENTS

PICTURES BY BEEK

LONDON
SAMPSON LOW, MARSTON & CO., LTD.
AND THE RICHARDS PRESS, LTD.

"I'VE COME TO BREAKFAST WITH YOU," SAID BIG-EARS
TO NODDY ONE DAY.

1. BIG-EARS HAS A PLAN

ONE morning, when little Noddy was still fast asleep in bed, somebody rode a bicycle up the path to his front door.

"Rat-a-tat-a-tat!" Somebody banged so hard on the knocker that little Noddy woke up in a hurry and almost fell out of bed in fright.

His little wooden head began to nod madly. "Oh dear—who's that knocking? I was fast asleep."

"Rat-a-tat-a-TAT-TAT!"

"Come in, come in, come in!" shouted Noddy, beginning to dress in a hurry.

The door burst open and in came Big-Ears, Noddy's friend. He had left his little bicycle outside, and he was smiling all over his face.

"Oh, it's you, Big-Ears," said Noddy in surprise. "I thought it must be somebody who wanted

7

me to drive them somewhere in my little car in a great hurry. What do you want to come banging on my door like that for, so early in the morning?"

"I've come to breakfast with you because I've thought of a plan," said Big-Ears. "Do hurry up and dress, Noddy. I'll get the breakfast and then I'll tell you about my plan."

Noddy put on his blue shorts, his red shirt, and tied his yellow scarf round his neck. He began to feel rather excited. Big-Ears' plan must be a good one if he had to come to breakfast!

Big-Ears found two eggs and began to boil them. He cut some bread-and-butter. "Where's your milk?" he said.

"Oh, I drank it all up last night," said Noddy. "The milkman will be here in a minute."

Sure enough there came a shout outside the door. "Milko! Milko!"

Big-Ears went to the door. "Two bottles of milk, please," he said. The milkman gave them to him. Big-Ears put his hand into his pocket

8

to get some money. Noddy called out at once.

"No, Big-Ears, no—that's not how I pay the milkman. Come in, milkman, and take your payment."

The milkman walked in with a grin and tapped Noddy's little head smartly. It began to nod very quickly indeed.

"Payment for one bottle," said the milkman. He tapped Noddy's head again as soon as it began to stop nodding and made it nod again, up and down, up and down.

"Payment for *two* bottles," he said. "Thank you. Good day!"

"Good gracious! Is that how you pay for your milk?" said Big-Ears in great surprise. "I wish *I* had a nodding head and could pay like that."

9

"Well, the milkman just loves to nod my head as fast as he can," said Noddy, tying up his shoes. "I have to pay him a lot more nods for cream, though—it's not so cheap as milk."

"Come along—breakfast is ready," said Big-Ears. "Do hurry up, Noddy— you've washed, you've cleaned your teeth, you've done your hair. I simply can't wait to tell you my plan."

Noddy sat down and tapped his egg hard on the top. "Now tell me," he said. "Is it a BEE-OOOO-TI-FUL one?"

"Yes," said Big-Ears. "I've come to say that we ought to have a holiday—and we ought to go to the seaside—at once, this very day, because it's such lovely weather. We can paddle——"

"What's paddle?" said Noddy, looking excited. "And where's the seaside? And what is it?"

"Oh, Noddy—I keep forgetting how little you know!" said Big-Ears. "The seaside is a lovely place. It's got heaps of yellow sand and a lot of blue water, and you dig in the sand and paddle in

THE MILKMAN TAPPED NODDY'S HEAD AND MADE IT
NOD UP AND DOWN, UP AND DOWN.

the water. And you go right into it, too—up to your neck, if you like."

"I don't like," said Noddy, looking rather scared. "I don't even go up to my neck in the bath."

"Oh, don't be silly, Noddy," said Big-Ears. "You'll love it all. Everyone likes holidays."

"They sound sort of prickly," said Noddy, finishing up his egg.

Big-Ears laughed and laughed. "Not *holly*-days made of prickly *holly*!" he said. "Oh dear, you're always so nice and silly, Noddy. Will you come? We can go together today in your little car."

"Oh *yes*—I'll come anywhere with you, dear Big-Ears, because you are my friend," said Noddy, beaming at him. "Let's leave all the washing-up and go to the seaside at once, now, this very minute, immediately!"

2. OFF TO THE SEASIDE

BIG-EARS wouldn't go till they had washed-up, made Noddy's bed and put everything tidy.

"There—your little house looks nice," he said. "Noddy, put your pyjamas into a bag, and your tooth-brush, sponge, soap and flannel. And take the money that is in your money-box. I've got mine, too—quite a lot."

Noddy began to feel very excited indeed. He took out his money and gave it to Big-Ears to keep safely for him. He patted his little bed and said goodbye to it.

"I wish I could take you with me, bed," he said. "Goodbye till I come back again. Big-Ears, do we sleep in beds at the seaside?"

"No. I've got another plan about that," said Big-Ears. "You'll love it. Now stop saying goodbye to everything, Noddy, and come along. Listen—there's your little car hooting for you in its garage!"

"Parp-parp-parp!" Yes, that was Noddy's little car, longing to be taken out into the sunshine for a drive.

Big-Ears and Noddy went out, and Noddy slammed his front door behind him. He got out his dear little car and drove it on to the roadway. Big-Ears wheeled out his bicycle.

"Are you going to ride to the seaside on your bicycle?" said Noddy in surprise.

"No. It's too far," said Big-Ears. "I'll tie it on at the back of the car."

So he did, and here they go together in Noddy's little car through the streets of Toyland. How excited they look!

Miss Fluffy Cat waved her sunshade at Noddy. "Stop! Stop, Noddy! I want you to take me to the station!" she cried.

"Can't stop, can't stop!" shouted Noddy.

"STOP! STOP! NODDY!" CRIED MISS FLUFFY CAT. "I WANT
YOU TO TAKE ME TO THE STATION!"

15

"I'm taking myself to the seaside for a holiday."

And on he went at top speed. Then Mr. Wobbly Man hailed him. "Hi, Noddy! Stop! I want a lift."

"Can't stop, can't stop! I'm off to the seaside!" shouted Noddy.

"Parp-parp!" said the little car excitedly and jerked high into the air over a rut in the road.

"Tell the car to be sensible," said Big-Ears. "There goes my hat—jerked right off my head! Stop, car, STOP!"

The car stopped with such a jolt that Big-Ears fell out. "I'm sorry, I'm sorry, I'm sorry!" said Noddy, very fast. "That's the worst of this car—it always gets excited when I do."

Big-Ears picked up his hat from the road and got back into the car. They went off again, and little Noddy began to sing.

16

"We're off to the sea,
  Big-Ears and me.
  We'll dig in the sand;
  Oh, won't it be grand!
  We'll paddle and play,
  Oh, hip-hip-hurray!"

"That's a nice song," said Big-Ears. "You're very good at making up songs, Noddy. Let's both sing that one together."

So they began to sing it at the tops of their voices, and the car joined in. "Par-par-par-par-parp!" Then it gave a leap of joy, and Big-Ears almost lost his hat again. There was a loud noise at the back of the car and then a crash.

Big-Ears looked round, startled. Then he gave a shout. "Stop, Noddy, stop! My bicycle's fallen off! We're leaving it behind. STOP, I tell you!"

Noddy stopped. "I'm sorry, I'm sorry, I'm sorry!" he began, but Big-Ears really was cross this time. He ran to pick up his bicycle.

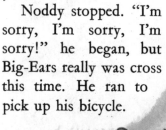

Was it hurt or broken?
No, thank goodness, it wasn't!

"I think I'll carry it round my shoulders," said Big-Ears, getting back into the car. "I just couldn't *bear* to lose my little bicycle. There—I'm ready. And please do drive properly, Noddy. We'll never get to the seaside if we keep dropping things into the road."

"Your bicycle wheel is sticking into my neck," said Noddy. "I can't nod my head."

"Well, never mind," said Big-Ears. "It will

be a nice change for your head not to nod. Look out, Noddy—you nearly went into that cow!"

"It's so very difficult to drive with a wheel sticking into my neck," said Noddy, and he nearly bumped into another cow. "Oh dear! Did you see how that cow jumped? It must be the one that was clever enough to jump over the moon!"

That made Big-Ears laugh, and he nearly dropped his bicycle. Then he gave a shout that almost made Noddy drive into some Noah's Ark animals.

"Look—a sign-post! And it says TO THE SEASIDE. We're nearly there, Noddy; we're nearly there!"

3. THE SEASIDE IS LOVELY!

NODDY drove on and on—and then he suddenly stopped the car and stared. "What's that?" he said, pointing to a big, moving mass of bright blue.

"It's the sea," said Big-Ears, excited. "Isn't it lovely!"

"It's too big," said Noddy. "Much too big. Let's go and find a dear little sea. This one's too big and it keeps moving. And what are those things that keep rising up to look at us and then falling over with a big splash?"

"They're only waves," said Big-Ears. "Drive on, Noddy. Get nearer."

Noddy drove down on to the yellow sand. He got out and stared at the big blue sea. He dug his feet into the soft, warm sand.

"Where does the sea end?" he said. "It goes on and on and on and on and . . ."

"Don't bother about where it ends," said Big-Ears. "It *begins* here, anyway. Come on—let's paddle."

"I don't know how to," wailed Noddy. "And I still think the sea's too big. *Please*, Big-Ears, let's go and find a small sea."

"You're silly," said Big-Ears, and took off his shoes and socks. He turned up his trousers and ran down to the sea. He splashed in the little white-edged waves and shouted for joy.

"It's lovely, it's lovely! Come and paddle, Noddy, and make a song about it. Oh, do come and feel the water in between your toes!"

Noddy suddenly thought he would. He ran to the sea at top speed, and Big-Ears *just* managed to stop him before he went in with his shoes on. Noddy sat down and took them off.

Then he ran to join Big-Ears, and the two of them paddled up and down, up and down, making splashes as they went.

"This is better than splashing in puddles after the rain," said Noddy joyfully. "There's much more water to splash with. Oooh—*that* was a big splash, wasn't it, Big-Ears? Did I wet you?"

"Yes, you did," said Big-Ears. "Look out—there's quite a big wave coming."

Noddy jumped up and down in the wave joyfully, and sang at the top of his voice:

" The sea is big,
  The sea is blue,
  It's big enough
  For me and you,
  It's big enough for
    everybody—
  Come and splash with
    little Noddy!"

Noddy jumped so high that he suddenly fell over—SPLASH! There he was, lying in the water, very surprised and rather frightened.

THERE WAS NODDY LYING IN THE WATER, VERY
SURPRISED AND RATHER FRIGHTENED.

"Oh, I'm wet! Oh, the sea's cold! Oh, there's a wave running over me! Help, Big-Ears, help!"

Big-Ears helped him up. "You're wet through," he said. "I knew that would happen. I shall take you back home if you do silly things, Noddy."

"Oh no, no, no!" shouted Noddy, beginning to splash about again. "The seaside is lovely, lovely, lovely!"

4. SOMEWHERE TO SLEEP

"WHERE are we going to live?" asked Noddy, when they sat down to dry their feet on Big-Ears' enormous handkerchief. "Are there houses at the seaside?"

"Of course," said Big-Ears. "Look behind you, up on the cliff there. Lots of houses!"

"It's a long way up that cliff," said Noddy, looking at it. "And I want to be near the sea, Big-Ears. Let's live down here on the sand. I like it."

He ran his hands through the sand and threw some at Big-Ears. It went into his eyes and down his neck. He was very cross.

"Don't do that, Noddy," he said. "I can't see out of my left eye now. You're unkind."

"I didn't mean to be, I didn't, I didn't, I didn't!" said Noddy. "I won't do silly things any more, Big-Ears. Tell me where we are going to live. Can we live down here on the sand?"

"Well, I did think of getting a tent," said Big-Ears.

"Oh *yes*, Big-Ears, let's get a tent!" cried Noddy.

> "I always meant
> To live in a tent,
> Wherever I went."

"You *didn't*," said Big-Ears. "That's a silly song. Now I'll go and buy the tent. We can make two nice holes in the sand for beds, and another hole to keep our things in—and the tent will give us a fine roof."

"I'll make the holes while you get the tent," said Noddy. "What shall I make the holes with?"

"Scrape them out with your hands," said Big-Ears. "I'll bring back spades and pails for us—and shrimping nets—and perhaps a little ship to sail on a pool."

"Oh, Big-Ears, I *do* like being at the sea-side!" said Noddy, and he began to scrape hard in the sand. "I'll make some lovely beds for us here in the sand. Hurry up and get the tent."

Big-Ears went walking up the beach to the steps that led up the side of the steep cliff to the little village above. Noddy worked hard while he was gone. He made two nice holes, and lay down in each to make sure they were the right size. Then he made a hole to keep their things in. He put his bag there and Big-Ears' bag as well.

Big-Ears came back just as Noddy had finished his work. He had so many parcels that it was quite difficult to see Big-Ears himself!

"Tent!" he said, throwing down a big parcel. "Spades. Pails. Nets. Bathing-suits. Ship. Sandwiches. Biscuits. Lemonade."

"Good gracious, Big-Ears! Have you spent all our money?" cried Noddy.

"Not quite," said Big-Ears, and began to undo the parcel that held the tent. Soon he was shaking out the little tent and sorting out the small poles and ropes that went with it.

NODDY TRIED TO PUT UP THE TENT, BUT IT KEPT
FALLING DOWN ON HIM.

Noddy tried to put up the tent, but it kept falling down on him. "Let *me* do it, Noddy," said Big-Ears, and he did it very well indeed, as you can see. It was a dear little tent.

They crawled inside it. "This is *my* bed," said Noddy, getting into one sand-hole. "And that's yours, Big-Ears. Oh, what fun this is!" He shut his eyes tightly.

"Don't go to sleep yet!" said Big-Ears. "It isn't night-time. Look, Noddy, I'm putting all the food into this hole where you've put the bags. The spades and pails and things can go outside on the beach with the car and my bicycle. Now— our holiday has begun!"

5. GO AWAY, SEA!

"IT'S tea-time," said Noddy, feeling for the
sandwiches. "We missed our dinner, and now
I'm very hungry for tea. Let's sit in the sand
outside the tent and have a big tea, Big-Ears.
Then we'll paddle. I like paddling. I shall paddle
all day long."

They sat down in the sand and began to eat
their tea. After that they took a spade each and
began to dig.

"I'll make a big castle," said Noddy. "The
biggest that ever was made."

"Mine will be bigger!" said Big-Ears. They
both worked very hard indeed and then sat down
for a rest. Noddy stared at the sea. He looked
very puzzled.

"Big-Ears," he said, "the sea is coming to look at our castles. It's creeping up the beach. It's getting nearer and nearer."

"So it is!" said Big-Ears, surprised too. "It was very far away from this spot when we arrived, wasn't it? Now it's quite close. Goodness me—do you suppose it really *is* coming to see what we've built?"

"Well, look—that last little wave almost reached your castle," said Noddy. "And now this next one is licking round it. Big-Ears, what shall we do? The sea might take our tent away!"

Big-Ears got up and pointed at the sea. "Go away, sea!" he said in a very stern voice. "Go away, I tell you! Do you hear me?"

Well, the sea didn't take any notice at all. It ran all round Big-Ears' castle and then it began to lap at Noddy's. "It's nibbling it away," said Noddy. "Go away, sea! GO AWAY!"

"Look, there are some toys over there digging

"GO AWAY, SEA!" SAID BIG-EARS IN A VERY STERN VOICE.
"GO AWAY, I TELL YOU! DO YOU HEAR ME?"

in the sand," said Big-Ears. "I'll go and ask them to do something about this annoying sea."

So he went over to two little golliwogs, a teddy-bear and a pink pig, all playing together in the sand.

"Ha ha, ho ho! He says the sea came up to look at his castle and won't go away!" laughed the teddy-bear. "Just you tell it to go back, Brownie!"

"I did," said Big-Ears. "But it took no notice. We're afraid it will take away our tent."

"No, it won't," said a small doll sitting in a nearby deck-chair. "The tide will go out again in a minute."

"What's the tide?" asked Big-Ears, who had never heard that the sea runs right up the beach and right down again, day after day. He just thought it always stayed in the same place.

"You'll soon learn!" said the little doll. Then Big-Ears heard Noddy shouting to him.

"Big-Ears, Big-Ears! It's all right. The sea is doing what you told it and it's going away again. Come and see!"

Sure enough, Noddy was right. The sea had left the sand-castles and was gradually going down the beach away from them. The tide was going out!

"You are very, very clever, Big-Ears," said Noddy. "Even the sea does what you tell it! I am so glad to have a clever friend like you!"

That night they both went to sleep in the little tent. It was warm and comfortable in their sand-beds. Big-Ears tied back the flap of the tent so that they could see the stars peeping down.

"I can hear the sea singing its own song," said Noddy sleepily. "It's a nice song. It goes like this:

> Here I run a little way.
>   Back again I go;
> Now I'm coming up the sand
>   To catch your little toe.
> Splishy-splashy-splishy-splash,
>   What a noise I make!
> All the night I never stop,
>   I keep you wide awake!"

But the sea didn't keep Noddy and Big-Ears awake! They are both as fast asleep as can be— just look at them.

6. WHAT A LOVELY TIME!

NODDY and Big-Ears had such a wonderful time at the seaside. Once they built a most enormous castle, bigger than anyone else's, and Noddy sat on the top of it.

The tide came in and the sea swept all round the castle, but Noddy still sat there, shouting joyfully.

And then, oh dear, such a big wave came that it knocked the castle down and Noddy fell into the water. "Save me, save me! I'll drown! I can't swim!" he cried.

"Get up and walk, then!" shouted everybody. So Noddy stood up—and, will you believe it, the water was only up to his ankles! So he was quite safe after all, and he paddled quickly to the beach.

"Noddy, if you wet your clothes like this we shall have to wear bathing-suits all the time," said Big-Ears. So after that they wore their little bathing-suits, and Noddy liked his very much.

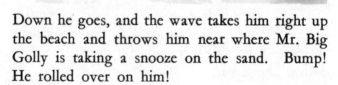

He went bathing in his suit and danced about madly. Look out, Noddy—here comes a very big wave! There, I knew he wouldn't see it!

Down he goes, and the wave takes him right up the beach and throws him near where Mr. Big Golly is taking a snooze on the sand. Bump! He rolled over on him!

Mr. Big Golly woke up with a jump and gave such a shout that Noddy fled away at top speed. He went to Big-Ears, almost crying.

"Tell the waves they're not to knock me over!" he said. "Tell them, Big-Ears."

But Big-Ears only laughed at him. "Get your shrimping net and come and catch shrimps with me," he said. So off they went with their nets, and caught a lot of little shrimps.

A kind sailor doll took the shrimps home to his wife and cooked them for Noddy and Big-Ears. Then they had shrimp sandwiches for their tea, and shared them with Miss Whiskers, a toy kitten, and Tiddles, her boy-cousin.

"Shrimps taste nice," said Noddy. "I'll catch some more."

"Crabs taste nice, too," said Tiddles. "You could catch some of those, perhaps, and then we'd have a crab tea."

"How do you catch crabs?" asked Noddy. But nobody knew.

"I'm going to paddle," said Noddy after tea. "I'm going to paddle right up to my waist!"

And off he went, going deeper and deeper into the sea. Then he suddenly gave a loud yell.

"Big-Ears! Oh, Big-Ears, save me! Something has got hold of my foot. BIG-EARS! Come quick. Oooooh!"

Big-Ears rushed into the sea at once, quite frightened. What was happening to little Noddy? Who was under the water, clutching at his foot?

Noddy fell over in the water when a big wave came. He screamed loudly. "Big-Ears, Big-Ears! Come quickly! Something has got me!"

Big-Ears waded to him, pulled him up, and carried him to the shore. Noddy was still squealing.

BIG-EARS WADED OUT TO NODDY, PULLED HIM UP, AND
CARRIED HIM TO THE SHORE. HE WAS STILL SQUEALING.

41

" My foot, my foot! Oh, something's got my foot!"

And, dear me, what was that hanging on to his foot? Why—a great big crab! Look at it, holding on with its claws, pinching poor Noddy hard.

Tiddles pulled it off —and how he laughed. "It's a crab! Oh, Noddy, you wanted to catch a crab, and you have!"

"I didn't catch it. It caught *me*!" wept Noddy, rubbing his foot. "Horrid crab! I'll cook you and have you for my supper! Oh, Big-Ears, it did pinch my foot!"

Big-Ears put a fine bandage on Noddy's foot. "Now I'll get that bad crab," said Noddy fiercely, standing up.

But the crab was nowhere to be seen! It had run off into a nearby pool, and nobody knew where it was. It didn't mean to be eaten for Noddy's supper.

"Well, you won't want to catch crabs again," said Miss Whiskers. "And mind you look out for lobsters, too, Noddy—they pinch worse than crabs."

"And don't you catch jellyfish," said Tiddles with a grin. "They sting."

"I don't think the seaside is such a very nice place after all," said Noddy sadly.

"Don't be silly," said Big-Ears. "You go and get your little ship and we'll sail it. You'll soon forget about the crab!"

So here they are, sailing the ship. It floats beautifully, and when the wind takes the sail the boat goes right to the very end of Noddy's string.

"It's perfectly plain
   You're happy again,"
said Big-Ears, and laughed.
" In fact I am sure
   You are happy once more!

There, Noddy—*I've* made up a little song this time. Aren't I clever?"

7. THE BRAVE LITTLE CAR

NOW one day the wind blew and clouds came over the sky. The sea was grey instead of blue, and the waves were so very big that Noddy was frightened of them. It was too cold to wear bathing-suits, so Noddy and Big-Ears wore all the clothes they had got.

"Look, Noddy!" said Big-Ears suddenly. "There is a boat out there on the rough sea. Who is in it? It looks like two small teddy-bears—and Miss Whiskers—and Tiddles, her cousin—and a doll. How silly of them to go boating on such a rough day!"

"Oh, Big-Ears—the boat is rocking to and fro! And look, that big wave went right over it!" cried Noddy. "Big-Ears, there will be a ship-

wreck—the boat will go over and sink to the bottom of the sea!"

"Oh dear! What can we do?" said Big-Ears. "Noddy—the boat *has* gone over—right over—and everyone is in the sea. Oh, WHAT shall we do?"

"I'll go and rescue them," said Noddy at once, but Big-Ears held on to him tightly.

"No—of course not. You'd be drowned, too. Nobody can stand up against those big waves."

"Oh, but, Big-Ears, look at the poor things tossing about in the water," wailed Noddy. "Oh, poor Tiddles—poor Miss Whiskers—poor——"

Then a noise behind them made them jump. "Parp-parp! Parp-parp!" And, will you believe it, Noddy's car rushed by them at top speed and ran straight into the water!

"Come back, come back!" shouted Noddy. But the brave little car took no notice. It plunged

into the big waves and drove itself through the sea to where the boat had turned over.

"It's got to Tiddles! He's climbing in!" cried Noddy, dancing up and down in joy. "Now he's helping little Miss Whiskers in! Now the car's gone to pick up the two small teddy-bears. . . ."

"And now it's gone to the little doll," said Big-Ears. "Oh, she can't climb in—there isn't room. Yes, there is! Tiddles has got her on his lap. Now the car's turning itself round again. . . ."

"It's coming back! It's rescued everybody!" cried Noddy. "Oh, my dear, brave little car!"

A lot of people were now on the beach watching. How they cheered and shouted when the little car ran up the sand with all the shipwrecked toys quite safe.

"Parp-parp!" it said proudly. "Parp-parp!"

"Oh, Miss Whiskers, your fur is so wet," said Noddy. He got a towel to dry her. Everyone crowded round, talking and cheering. Hurrah! The brave little car had saved everyone. It stood

THE BRAVE LITTLE CAR DROVE ITSELF THROUGH THE SEA
TO WHERE THE BOAT HAD TURNED OVER.

there, dripping wet, saying "Parp-parp!" whenever anyone patted it.

The toys were taken to their homes to be dried and put to bed to get over their shock. Noddy and Big-Ears dried the little car. Then Noddy wheeled it to its usual place on the beach. It made a curious creaking noise and went very slowly.

"Being in the sea-water hasn't done it any good," said Big-Ears. "What a pity! Oh dear! I wish this wind would stop blowing. I'm so afraid that my two big ears will be blown away."

"Let's get into the tent," said Noddy. "If the wind gets much blowier we'll find ourselves up in the sky. My goodness—I daren't leave hold of my hat!"

48

8. A HORRID NIGHT

NOW that night wasn't at all nice. The wind blew very loudly and roughly. It blew sand into the tent. It blew a big wave right into the opening, and Noddy got his feet wet.

He was very angry. "What do you mean by coming into our tent, sea?" he said. "You've never done that before. Wind, be quiet. You're making such a noise that I can't go to sleep!"

But the wind wouldn't be quiet. It howled. It wailed. It shouted round the tent and pulled at the ropes that held it safe.

The tent shook and shivered, and so did Big-Ears and Noddy. "I wish we were back at home in my dear little house," said Noddy. "Or in your toadstool house, Big-Ears. I do really."

And then just as he said that something happened. The wind pounced down on the tent, pulled out all the ropes, and whipped the whole tent away into the night! Just fancy that!

Noddy and Big-Ears didn't know what had happened for a minute. They suddenly felt very cold—and then Big-Ears saw the stars in the sky above him!

"Our tent's gone!" he cried. "Noddy, the wind has taken away our tent!"

Noddy put out his hand to feel the tent, but it wasn't there, of course. All he did was to put his finger into Big-Ears' eye by mistake.

"Oh! I'm sorry, I'm sorry, I'm sorry!" he said. "Oh, Big-Ears, I'm frightened. Our tent is gone. Can I please cuddle up to you in case I'm blown away, too?"

"Yes," said Big-Ears, and he let Noddy creep into his kind, friendly arms. The wind blew roughly over them, and the bell at the end of Noddy's hat tinkled loudly all the time. It really was a very horrid night.

" OH, BIG-EARS, I'M FRIGHTENED," CRIED NODDY. " OUR
TENT IS GONE."

In the morning Big-Ears sat up and looked round. Was the car safe? Yes, there it was, looking very miserable. It made a strange noise when Big-Ears looked at it. He awoke Noddy.

"Noddy—I think the car's got a bad cold. I'm sure it's trying to cough. Poor thing, it's been standing out all night in this dreadful cold wind —after getting a soaking yesterday when it rescued those toys from the sea."

"Oh dear!" said Noddy, sitting up, too. "Is there any sign of our tent, Big-Ears?"

"No. It's gone for ever, I'm sure," said Big-Ears sadly. "But we've still got the car—and my bicycle is safe. It's half-buried in sand—look."

"What a horrid, horrid night," said Noddy. "Big-Ears, what are we going to do? Please think hard. You're the clever one, you know. What are we going to do?"

9. HOME AGAIN, HURRAH!

BIG-EARS pulled his hat down hard so that the wind couldn't whip it off his head.

"We're going home," he said. "That's what we are going to do, little Noddy. Our holiday is over, and it's time to go back."

"Of course! Why didn't I think of that, too?" said Noddy joyfully. "Home again—how lovely that will be!"

"You see, the weather isn't nice for living out-of-doors in a tent any more," said Big-Ears.

"And we haven't got a tent now," said Noddy.

"And our money has come to an end," said Big-Ears.

"So we must go home and earn some more," said Noddy. "That will be nice. It's good to work hard and earn lots of money."

"And your car is still very wet, and has caught a dreadful cold," said Big-Ears.

"Yes—and I really ought to clean it well, and look at its insides to put them right," said Noddy. "Oughtn't I, little car?"

"Pooooooo-ooooop!" said the car, in a very hoarse, sad voice. It couldn't even say "Parp-parp!"

"Well, it seems to me that it would be a very good and exciting thing to go back home," said Big-Ears. "We've had a lovely time, but that's come to an end. We'll say goodbye to all our friends here and leave this morning."

So they piled their luggage into the little car, tied Big-Ears' bicycle firmly to the back so that it wouldn't fall off, and said goodbye to all their friends.

"Goodbye! We'll come again another time!" called Noddy and Big-Ears.

"Goodbye! And goodbye, dear little car, too!" called everyone. "Hurry up and get rid of your cold."

"Pooo-ooo-pooooop!" said the car bravely, and went off rather slowly. Big-Ears' bicycle was quite safe this time, because the little car didn't feel well and simply could *not* go fast!

And then at last they got home. The car said "Poooo-oooop!" quite loudly when it saw its own little garage again, and the noise made Mr. and Mrs. Tubby Bear look out of their window. How excited they were to see Noddy and Big-Ears back again!

"Oh, how we've missed you!" they cried, hugging them both. "Did you have a nice holiday? Oh, we must have a tea-party this very afternoon to welcome you home!"

Noddy went into his little house. It did look so nice. "My own little House-for-One," he said. "I've come back, and I won't go away again for a long time. I really won't."

Well, the news soon went round that Noddy and Big-Ears had come home again, and how excited everyone was!

Miss Fluffy Cat came with a big bunch of flowers. Mr. Wobbly Man came with some ripe plums. Big Jumbo arrived with a new chocolate cake balanced carefully on the tip of his trunk. Monkey came with an enormous bottle of home-made lemonade.

"Oh, really—everyone is so kind!" said Noddy, almost crying for joy. "Why did we go away from such kind friends, Big-Ears?"

"To have a holiday, of course," said Big-Ears.

"It was nice having a holiday—and it's nice coming home again. Noddy, your little car is better already. I heard it say 'Parp-parp!' quite properly just then. I expect it feels happy to be back in its own garage."

57

"I think we ought to ask all your friends to our little tea-party and make it a big one," said kind Mrs. Tubby Bear, seeing all the presents that kept arriving. "Then everyone can share in your welcome-home."

So now they are having a perfectly wonderful tea-party, and Noddy and Big-Ears are as happy as can be. Even Mr. Plod the policeman came, and when he heard about the lost tent he promised to do his best to get it back.

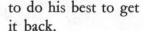

"But if he gets it back, don't you go rushing off on holiday again!" said Mr. Golly.

"Oh no, I won't," said little Noddy happily. "I don't feel as if I EVER want to go away again now. You're all so kind. Oh dear—there's a song coming—I can feel it!"

"Let it come," said Big-Ears, smiling, and Noddy stood up and sang:

NOW THEY ARE HAVING A PERFECTLY WONDERFUL TEA-PARTY, AND NODDY AND BIG-EARS ARE AS HAPPY AS CAN BE.

'How nice it is to go away
And have a lovely holiday;
And yet although it's fun to roam,
It's even better coming home,
Coming home—
Coming home—
It's really LOVELY coming home!"

Well—that was a good song for an ending,
wasn't it? How *does* Noddy think of his songs?
No wonder everyone is clapping him and calling
for more.

Good old Noddy—we'll hear about you some
other time, so have some more adventures, won't
you?

LOOK
FOR THE
NEXT
NODDY
BOOK